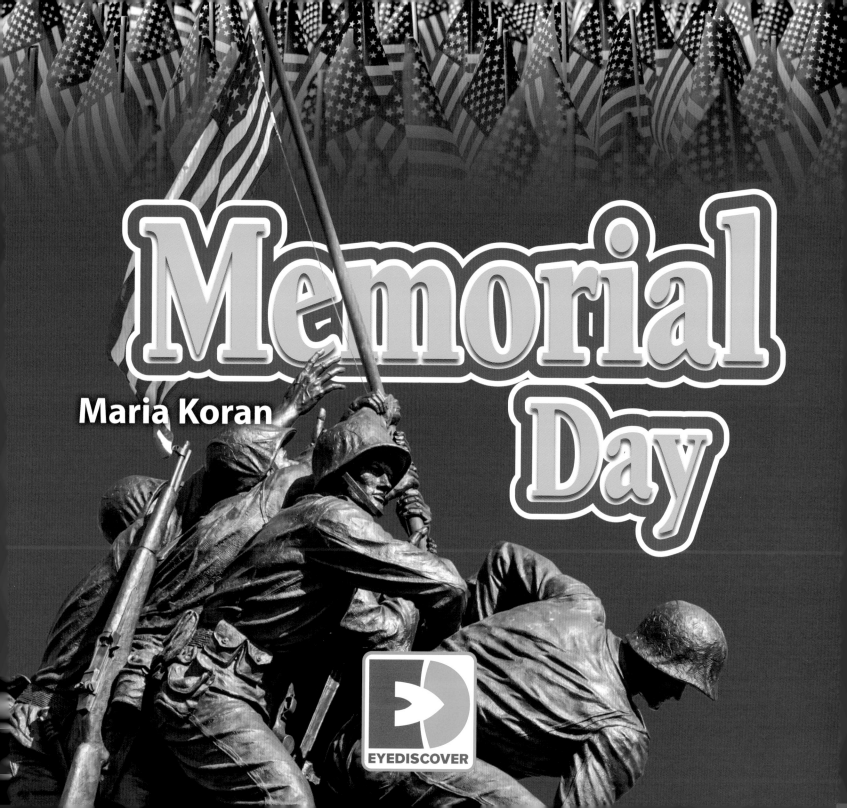

Memorial Day

Maria Koran

EYEDISCOVER

EYEDISCOVER

Go to **www.eyediscover.com** and enter this book's unique code.

BOOK CODE

AVT26996

EYEDISCOVER brings you optic readalongs that support active learning.

Published by AV² by Weigl
350 5th Avenue, 59th Floor New York, NY 10118
Website: www.eyediscover.com

Library of Congress Control Number: 2019946304

ISBN 978-1-7911-0814-4 (hardcover)

Printed in Guangzhou, China
1 2 3 4 5 6 7 8 9 0 23 22 21 20 19

072019
121818

Project Coordinator: John Willis
Designers: Mandy Christiansen and Ana María Vidal

Weigl acknowledges Alamy, Getty Images, and iStock as the primary image suppliers for this title.

EYEDISCOVER provides enriched content, optimized for tablet use, that supplements and complements this book. EYEDISCOVER books strive to create inspired learning and engage young minds in a total learning experience.

I am a lion.

Watch
Video content brings each page to life.

Browse
Thumbnails make navigation simple.

Read
Follow along with text on the screen.

Listen
Hear each page read aloud.

Your EYEDISCOVER Optic Readalongs come alive with...

Audio
Listen to the entire book read aloud.

Video
High resolution videos turn each spread into an optic readalong.

OPTIMIZED FOR

☑ **TABLETS**

☑ **WHITEBOARDS**

☑ **COMPUTERS**

☑ **AND MUCH MORE!**

Memorial Day

In this book, you will learn about

- what it is

- why we celebrate it

- how we celebrate it

and much more!

3

Memorial Day is on the last Monday in May. It is a day to remember those who died in war.

Memorial Day is also a time to honor the men and women who protect the United States.

Memorial Day was first held to honor the soldiers who died during the Civil War.

Many American cities have memorials for soldiers who fought in the Civil War.

MICHAEL D TERRY · JOHN D A ... ER · JOHN W BROOKS · CHARLE
WILLIE F CATO · MICHAEL R DZIENGEL ... Thomas A FRITZER Jr · JOHN K
· JOHN A LEE · RON ... MART ... D R OSBORNE · KEITH A P ...
· JOHN P PICKETT ... WHEELER · ERNEST
· FRANK N WILLIAMS · W ... AMIE L CAS ...
· HENRY M GNAN ...
· DOUGLAS A ...
JACKIE LEE SWINK · DO ...
· GEORGE R AN ...
· LAWRENCE ...
DANIEL G RULISO ... P S ... ARS ... VID, T ...
R BOOTH · AMIE D BROW ...
DAVID L JOLIET ... NE · EDWARD L GOODMAN · ROBERT ...
· RAYMOND ... K PRICE · DENN S M RATT N · MICHAEL K ...
· HAROLD ... RATTIN G R ... ICHA L E COTES · MARC ...
RIC ... EONARD D CO ...
WILLIAM T H ...
STE ... OAKFIELD ALABAMA
E ... F WALKE ...
ALLEN F K ...
JIMMY L SMITH ... H
A ...
· LARRY ...
RICHA ...
ALLEN W DUMKE ...
· BENNY C JA ...
JOSE ESPIRIDION ...
WILLIAM V W ST ...
· JESSI ...
JOHN L ESPENSHIEL ...
· BUDDY E HEN ...
· DALE F O ...
... MP SON

12

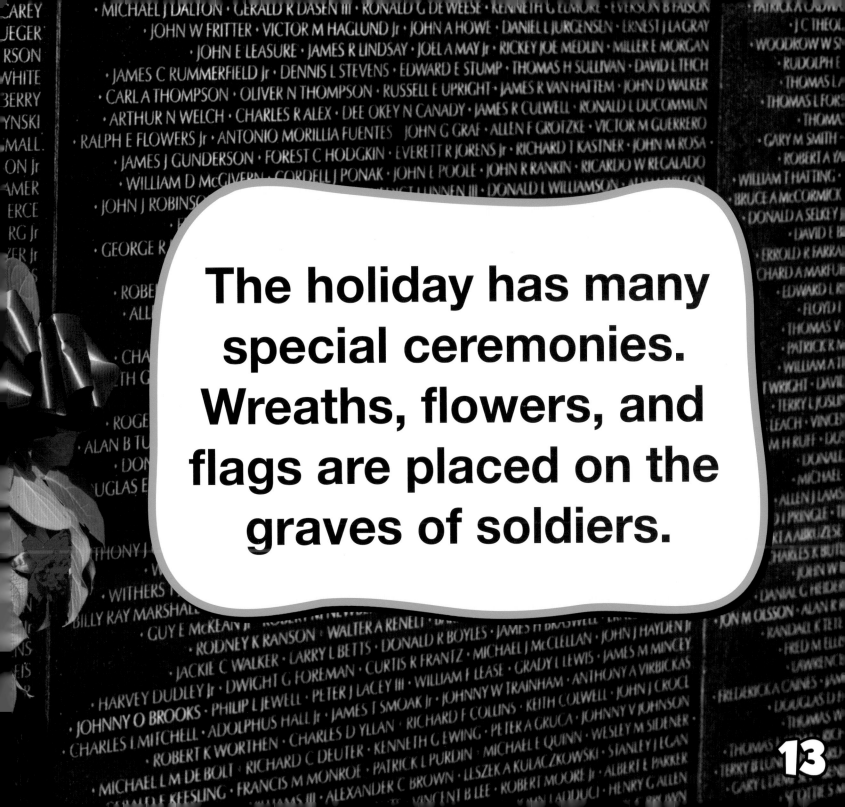

The holiday has many special ceremonies. Wreaths, flowers, and flags are placed on the graves of soldiers.

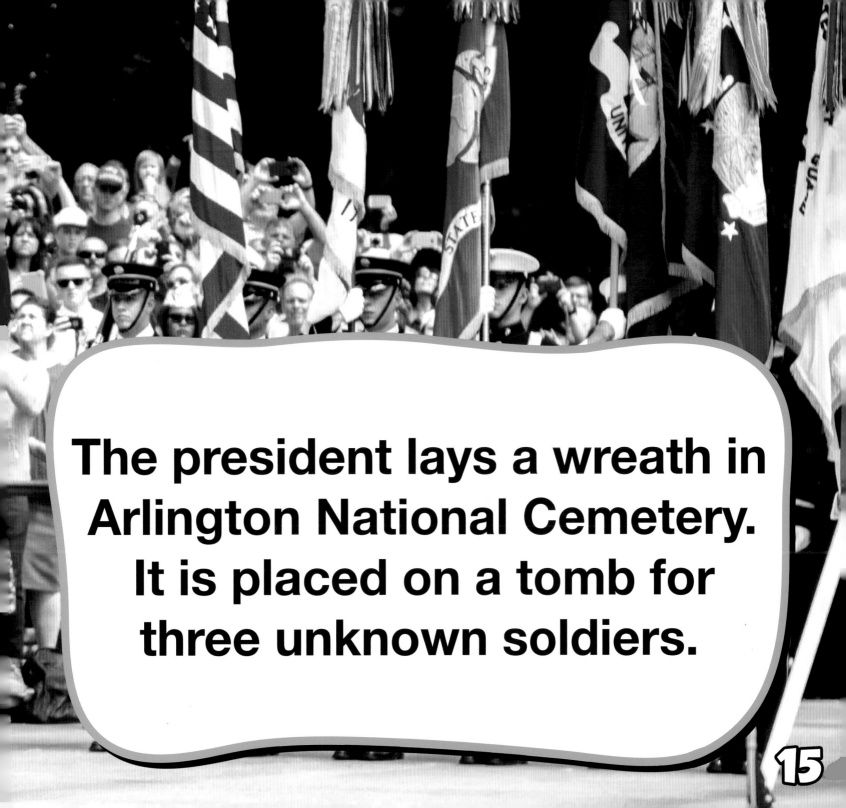

The president lays a wreath in Arlington National Cemetery. It is placed on a tomb for three unknown soldiers.

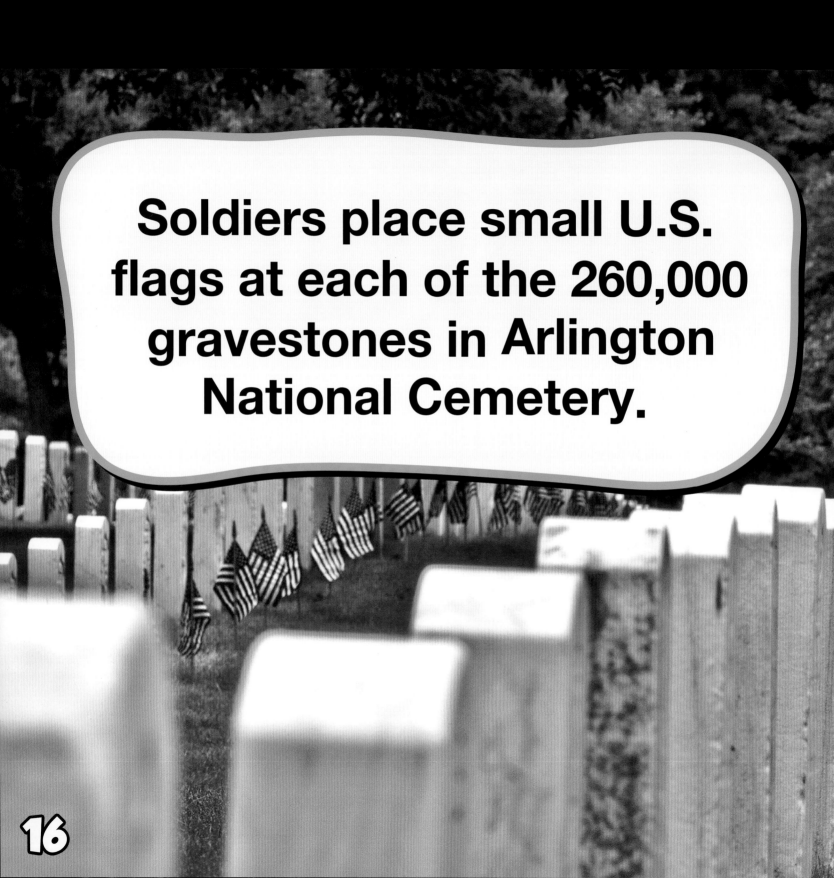

Soldiers place small U.S. flags at each of the 260,000 gravestones in Arlington National Cemetery.

Flags are flown at half-staff on government buildings.

19

At 3 p.m., all U.S. citizens are to stop for one minute of silence or listen to a song called "Taps."

21

MEMORIAL DAY FACTS

The name **Memorial Day** became **official** in **1971**.

A large concert is held in **Washington, D.C. each year** for Memorial Day.

Since **1990,**
millions of viewers
watch the
National Memorial Day Concert
on TV.

The **Tomb** of the **Unknown**
soldier is a symbol of **soldiers**
who have **died for their country.**

"**Taps**" is played on an
instrument called
a **bugle.**

23

KEY WORDS

Research has shown that as much as 65 percent of all written material published in English is made up of 300 words. These 300 words cannot be taught using pictures or learned by sounding them out. They must be recognized by sight. This book contains 36 common sight words to help young readers improve their reading fluency and comprehension. This book also teaches young readers several important content words, such as proper nouns. These words are paired with pictures to aid in learning and improve understanding.

Page	Sight Words First Appearance	Page	Content Words First Appearance
5	a, day, in, is, it, last, on, the, those, to, who	5	May, Memorial Day, Monday, war
6	also, and, men, states, time	6	United States, women
9	first, was	9	Civil War, soldiers
11	American, for, have, many, that	11	cities, memorials
13	are, has, of	13	ceremonies, flags, flowers, graves, holiday, wreaths
15	three	15	Arlington National Cemetery, president, tomb
16	at, each, place, small	16	gravestones
21	all, one, or, song, stop	19	buildings
		21	citizens, minute, silence, "Taps"

I am a lion.

Watch
Video content brings each page to life.

Browse
Thumbnails make navigation simple.

Read
Follow along with text on the screen.

Listen
Hear each page read aloud.

EYEDISCOVER

Go to www.eyediscover.com and enter this book's unique code.

BOOK CODE

AVT26996